FIGHT FIRE WITH FIRE

SIONNA FOX

FIGHT FIRE WITH FIRE
by Emily Kilduff
Copyright 2018

Praise for Sionna Fox

"Fight Fire with Fire"

This was faaaantastic…This one really went all out with tackling social issues, and the incorporation of body image was great.

-The Book Hammock

Bound To

Bound To is an erotic bittersweet coming of age romance…A full body read that flows along at a steady pacing with a witty banter, steamy sex scenes, and an engaging heroine whose initiation into BDSM opens the door to infinite possibilities if only she can accept she is worthy of it all.

-Smexy Books

I absolutely flipping love this book!....there is something about this one, in particular, that had me completely glued to my Kindle. Ms. Fox hit a home run with this one!

-Behind Closed Doors Book Reviews

Every encounter is...highlighted by the heady entice-
ment of finally exploring what feels right to Jolene,
not just good. Bound To was at its best when
reminding us that getting to know who we really are
might alter the person we always thought we were—
and that's okay.

-That's What I'm Talking About

Dark Rooms

It was hot, cold, tragic, vibrant, intoxicating, sexy,
ouchy, fun, and entertaining and not necessarily in
that order.

-The Romance Reviews, Top Pick

Dark Rooms was a hot 4 star read.

-Alpha Book Club

The illicit affair is sizzling hot and grabs the reader's
attention for a delightful adult read.

-Night Owl Reviews

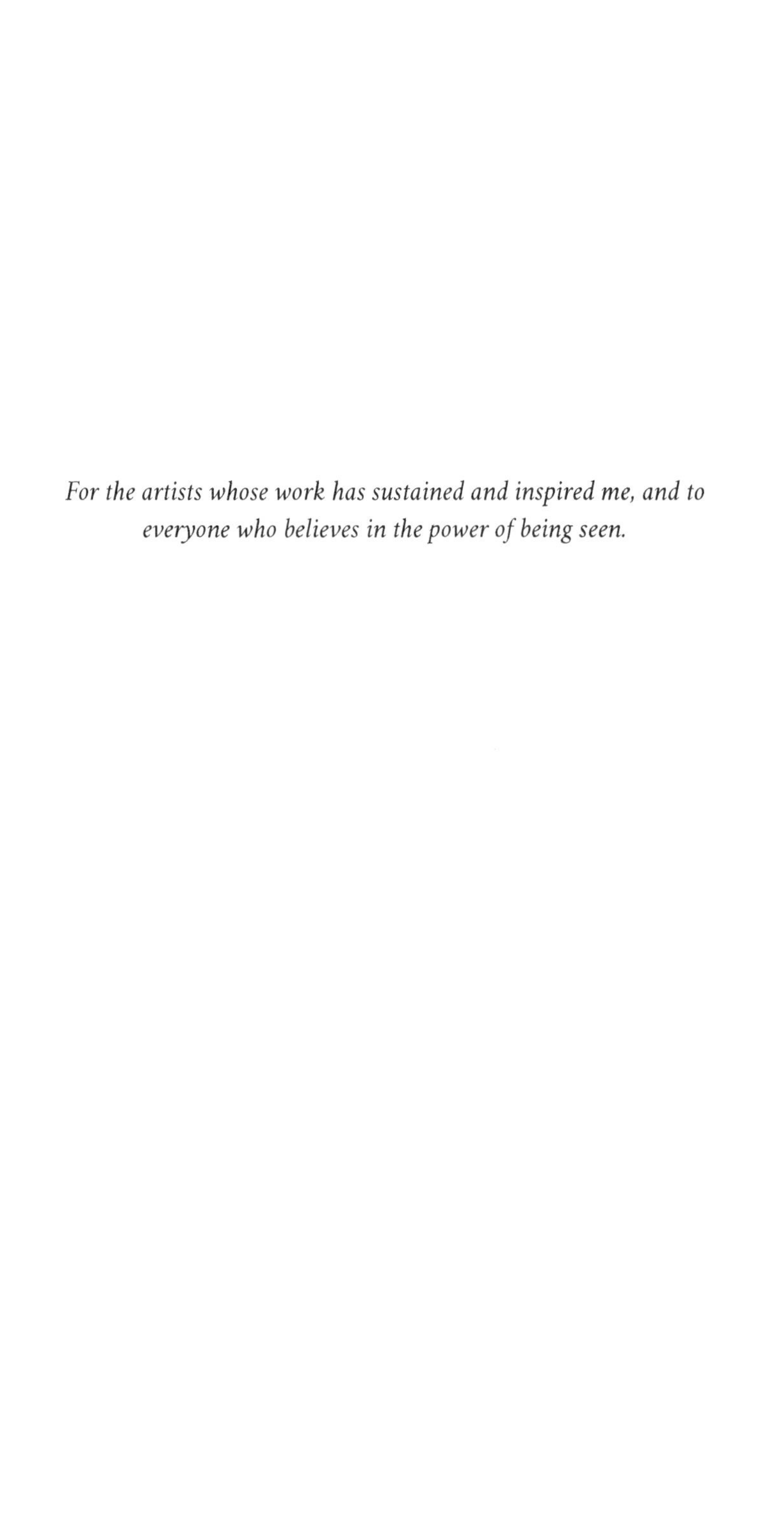

For the artists whose work has sustained and inspired me, and to everyone who believes in the power of being seen.

Chapter One

"I KNOW how to write a fucking grant, Larry." Frannie slammed the door to her office. The muffled thump of old wood catching on the door frame was not nearly as satisfying as she wanted it to be. The board had hired her to drag the museum into the twenty-first century, increase attendance and ticket sales to special exhibitions, and bring in new corporate donors—all of which she could and would do—but it would be so much easier if they didn't fight her every step of the fucking way.

Hell, she'd proven that by securing the region's only showing of the collected works of the late Rian Sampson, and the grant money to get the thing up on the walls. She'd even managed to get funding that was tied to educational opportunities by devising a program for low-income high school students to view the exhibition and learn about youth culture documentary. Basically they were going to let a bunch of teenagers run around the museum taking selfies, but they'd learn that teenagers had been doing that pretty much since the invention of the camera.

While she should have been basking in the success of

scoring the show from a highly competitive field of appli-
cants and working with the installers to draft plans for the
temporary walls they were going to need—Sampson's
catalog was enormous considering their brief professional
career—she'd been in a board meeting, defending her ability
to get the funding for next year's schedule.

They didn't trust her yet. But they would. This season
was going to put their little regional museum back on the
map. For years, they'd done nothing but bring in second-rate
touring exhibitions of stodgy classics, and their ticket sales
and membership numbers showed it. People were going to
notice them again, and bringing in Rian Sampson's work was
a major first step.

Sampson's work was a brilliant mash-up of documentary
and editorial, grit and glamour, their portrait subjects were
messy, their snapshots sharply composed. Grainy black and
white from basement punk shows mixed with lushly-colored
studio shots. And so many of them featured Ashley Patterson, muse, singer, activist, and erstwhile indie cool girl.

Frannie had been watching Sampson since their work
started appearing in small magazines, following them as they
moved into gallery shows while documenting their muse's
rise from belting her heart out in dirty basements to doing
the same in front of thousands. Through Sampson's lens,
Patterson was at turns fragile and confrontational, sweaty
and screaming into a microphone, then underlit and
exhausted, curled in on herself in the backseat of a van. They
were a powerful team, shaping the image of what it meant,
for that moment in time, to be young, to be queer, to be fat,
to be feminist, to be dirty and beautiful and to lift a middle
finger to anyone who wanted them to be otherwise.

When Sampson had died eight years earlier—a stupid,
senseless case of untreated pneumonia—Frannie had felt it
like the loss of a friend. To bring Sampson's work here, to

Frannie's hometown, to hold up a mirror for every closeted kid like the one she'd been, it was personal. For the first major show of her tenure, the first evidence of the changing face of the museum, to be the work of a queer artist— Frannie couldn't have dreamed of better. Approving the press packet that had just gone out had been a bittersweet triumph.

But before she could draft floor layouts for the exhibition space and talk to the permanent collections curator about making some changes to their installation to better lead attendees into Sampson's work, Frannie had to finish this section of another grant proposal so the board could hem and haw over whether she and the education director were out of their minds. They weren't. And she'd prove it.

Her door burst open, revealing her rather more harried than usual assistant. "Ms. Thorpe, you're gonna want to see this."

"For the last time, Holly, it's Frannie. What's wrong?"

She came around the desk with her phone in her hand and pressed play on a video from the local news station.

"What am I watching?"

"Just wait."

Frannie reflexively wrinkled her nose when the camera panned to Trenton Everett Markham III. He'd just announced a Senate run, invoking the bogeymen of immigrants, feminists, and queers to rile up his would-be constituents. A few years ago, she would never have taken his chances seriously. Now, he disgusted her at the same time as he struck fear in her heart. Their deep purple state could go either way, between rural conservatives convinced the government was coming for their guns and white suburbanites who wanted tax cuts, social services be damned. And Markham was holding up the museum schedule mailer that had gone out last weekend.

"Shit."

Through the tinny speakers of her phone, she heard him rail about public funding being used to spread filth in the community. The glorification of sin would not be tolerated on the public dime. This had to be stopped. The gay agenda was poisoning the youth. He ranted on at the shell-shocked local news host, and the producers let it go, seeing viral spread and dollar signs, Frannie was sure. She turned away from Holly's phone and put her head in her hands, dread roiling in her stomach.

Her desk phone rang.

She took a deep breath, straightened her glasses, smoothed the lapel of her blazer, and picked up. "Frances Thorpe, Special Exhibitions, how can I help you?"

"Have you seen the news?" Her boss didn't bother with a greeting. They'd all left the board meeting to the same video.

Frannie flipped over her phone. Notifications for the museum's social media accounts flashed across the screen every couple of seconds. This was bigger than local news. *Shit, shit, shit.*

"Yes, sir."

"This is not what the board meant when we talked about bringing additional publicity to the museum. There's talk of a boycott."

"Jonathan, the kind of people who are going to boycott this exhibition weren't going to come anyway. You know that. Right-wing Christian fundies were never our demographic. If anything, supporters will go out of their way to buy tickets for this." She could spin this. She could turn this around.

"And what about our funding? He's talking about curtailing the use of state and federal funding on arts programs. This is 1989 all over again. This is worse than 1989. They didn't have social media in 1989."

"They can't touch the public grants we already have for this year." She inhaled slowly. "And if we lose them next year, they only make up fifteen percent of our operating budget; we can make up the shortfall."

"Frances, they're talking about boycotting our corporate sponsors until they pull their support. They want to bury us."

"What? Where? All I saw was a bunch of posturing about public funding."

"It seems we've gone viral."

"Shit." In twenty years, from internships to slogging away in assistant curatorships, Frannie could count the number of times she'd been moved to curse at work. Most of them involved a hammer and her thumb when she used to pitch in with installation. "Sorry."

"Shit is right, Fran. This is not good."

"I'll fix it. I'll figure it out. We can make this work. Please don't make me pull the exhibition."

"I'm not going to ask you to. But that doesn't mean the board won't. You need to get in front of this, now."

"Okay. I know. I'm on it."

THERE WAS something perverse about still having a Google alert for your dead best friend, eight years after they'd died. But Ashley was officially the executor of Rian's estate, and while she could easily have delegated keeping tabs on where their name still popped up in the news, she hadn't.

It was bittersweet every time she saw the proof that Rian's legacy lived on. They'd never believed their work was made to last—"it's temporally fixed, Ash. The only thing it will be good for in a few years is nostalgia"— but Ashley never agreed. They used to argue about it all the time. Every shoot, every assignment, every magazine editorial, every snapshot of her hungover, or jet-lagged, or dancing her face off in some nameless club mattered. Evidence. A document. And she had been right in the end.

She'd rather have her best friend here with her to argue about it.

Rian thrived on confrontation. Look at me, see me; all of us weirdos exist and there is fuck-all you can do about it. Until they hadn't and all that was left was the work. Confronting people with it was Ashley's job now.

Her phone pinged. Curious, she followed the link to a local news channel, and watched, horrified as one Trenton Everett Markham III yelled at the bewildered host about the corruption of youth until he was red-faced and wild-eyed. He called on viewers to boycott the museum hosting an exhibition of Rian's work and promised, if elected, to eliminate funding for gay pornography masquerading as art.

Rian would have fucking loved it. Their very own Mapplethorpe moment. But Ashley's stomach sank.

She'd worked with Rian's former agent, gallery director, and primary collectors for over a year to make this tour happen. They'd pored over the applications of galleries and museums that wanted to host it. She'd campaigned to give it to the Briggs Museum of Art.

They were small, and the local population had historically limited access to contemporary art outside of a handful of small galleries that hosted a First Friday that was still heavily dominated by cishet artists working in traditional media. They needed something other than landscape paintings and the odd Rothko-esque color field. It was exactly the kind of small city that deserved access to Rian's work and Ashley had been impressed at the director's promise to get local kids into the exhibition through educational grants. Some kid was going to see themselves for the first time, the representation kids like her and Rian never had.

And they would be at risk of losing it.

Ashley suspected, based on the museum's history, the special exhibitions director was going to face major push-back from her board. They'd played it very boring and safe for years prior to appointing Frances Thorpe, and this was going to be too much change, too much controversy.

"Ash? You ready?" PJ, her bassist, peeked out from the booth where they'd been setting up to record. She hadn't even noticed they were waiting on her.

"Yeah, gimme a minute."

She tapped out a quick message to Rian's agent, asking him to get in touch with the museum and find out if they'd lost any sponsors and if there was anything they could do. She couldn't explain why, exactly, she was determined not to let Frances Thorpe lose the show. Something about the language of the application made Ashley suspect that Frances Thorpe needed this for herself and wanted it for the kid she had been. She bit her lip before adding, *Give Frances Thorpe my personal contact info. Tell her I'll do whatever I can to help.*

"Alright, let's go." She tossed her phone onto the couch and stepped into the booth.

Chapter Two

*W*ELL THAT'S JUST...INTERESTING.

Frannie had been dodging bullets in her inbox for days. Homophobic screeds full of spelling mistakes insisting that she was an agent of the devil turning the youth against god and threatening to expose her for what she was, to bring wrath and judgment down on her by letting her family and neighbors know she was a filthy homo. Which was…weirdly hilarious. A person would have to be incredibly clueless and straight to see Frannie, with her suits and her slight pompadour, and not immediately assume she was a lesbian.

Frannie had ditched hiding her own identity behind long hair and jeans and T-shirts and gone full dapper lesbian when she was in college. She'd been fortunate to have family who hadn't so much batted an eyelash when she came out as said, *we know, we were waiting for you to tell us, please let us buy you a suit that actually fits you for graduation.* Twenty years ago, that had still seemed like a big deal. For some it was still too much to hope for. But having these supposed warriors of god move from showing up on her digital doorstep and onto her literal one wasn't something grad school had prepared her for.

But this message was different. This message was from Rian Sampson's agent and contained personal contact details for Ashley Patterson. If Frannie's heart flip-flopped a bit, it was only because that meant they were aware of what was happening and they were nervous about the future of a show that was supposed to have a load-in in less than a month. It had nothing to do with having Ashley Patterson's contact info.

There was no time to fangirl. She was doing yet another interview this afternoon. She'd been told to get out in front of the mess and she was doing her damnedest, accepting any interview request that came from somewhere even half-way sympathetic. She was up to her eyeballs in journalists and bible-thumpers alike.

She took her glasses off to clean them, pushed her fore-lock out of her face, and straightened the collar of her shirt, using the chat window on her computer screen as a mirror while she waited for the producer on the other end to let her know they were ready to cut her in. The circles under her eyes looked harsh and dark in the grainy window. The late nights catching up on the work she was supposed to be doing all day while she struggled to put out the fire Trenton fucking Markham started were getting to her. And for as many interviews as she did, as many sympathetic outlets as she talked to, he was in front of conservative rags, on their talk shows, spouting off to anyone who would listen about the evils of governments funding gay pornography.

Poor Holly could barely keep up with the museum's social media accounts and had been driven to tears more than once by the awful things people said. Hell, Frannie was ten years older than she was, had years longer to toughen her skin against some of this shit, and she'd still cried more than once since this blew up.

At the producer's cue, she put her glasses back on, straightened her face into a carefully neutral, though slightly positive and inquisitive, expression she'd had to perfect with a quickness and faced the camera.

It was a blur of the same statements she'd been making. The museum believed in the value of the work. They were proud to bring a show like this into their community. This was art not pornography. There was a long, long history of provocation and social commentary in art. Public funding ensures the possibility of access for all; art shouldn't be a treat for only the wealthy. Seeing it in person, the scope, the size, the layout of the installation, the way individual pieces interact on a wall can't be replicated by online galleries or even books.

And then they pulled the rug out from under her.

"We've received word that Wilson Industries is pulling their funding for the show in light of the controversy. Does the museum have a statement?"

The look on the host's face in the chat window, the triumph of catching her off-guard with that news, would be burned into Frannie's brain for the rest of her life. Her jaw dropped, just for a second, but long enough that in the back of her mind she knew that fucking clip was going to be all over the goddamn conservative blogs within minutes.

She closed her mouth and cleared her throat. "We've certainly been grateful for their support in the past, and hope to continue our partnership on future projects. I have no further comment."

She was only vaguely aware of their thanking her for her time and signing off. She closed the video chat window, logged out of the program to be on the safe side, put her head on the desk and screamed.

Their single biggest financial backer was pulling their funding. They were fucked.

Jonathan opened the door. "You heard."

"On live television, no less."

"They sent out a press release, didn't even come to the board."

"Can they do that?"

"Their support is discretionary."

"Shit."

"Fran, we might—"

"No. We are not going to let Trenton fucking Markham win. I'll figure something out."

"It's a lot of money, Fran."

"I know. Goddammit, I know." Cursing at work was becoming the norm. "Look, Sampson's agent sent me an email. They're aware of the situation. Let me talk to them. Maybe we can fundraise. Give me a little time. Please."

It was a harebrained scheme at best, but if she could get Ashley Patterson on board…maybe. Fuck, if she'd really thought they were going to lose funding, she would have been giving a donor pitch with every interview and begging members for more money the second this thing broke. But they could catch up. Ashley could help.

"See what you can do."

"Just, tell the board we're working on it. We'll make up the shortfall."

Jonathan nodded grimly and left. Frannie opened her email, took a deep breath, and sent a desperate plea for help.

"Ah, fuck."

"What?"

"That museum in Wentworth lost one of their major sponsors."

"Shit. What are they gonna do?" PJ's practicality was a blessing sometimes, but it also made her a terrible person to vent to. And right now, Ashley wanted to vent.

Fucking puritanical fucks. Cowards. "I don't know. The special exhibitions person is talking about setting up a fundraising campaign, but that's never gonna make up the kind of shortfall they must be facing." She pulled on her ponytail. They were behind schedule in the studio. What she was about to say was stupid. She couldn't afford it. But something about *this* museum hosting *this* show, and with *this* woman at the head of it, made Ashley want to do something really stupid. "I think we should do a show."

"Ash, we're three days behind already. You don't have time to organize a show. Besides, no offense, but your tours mostly break even, dude."

"I know. I know. But I have to do something." She bit her lip and scrolled her contacts. "Work on the bridge of track seven, it was sloppy as shit on the last take. I'll be back in ten minutes."

She stepped into the hallway and dialed the number.

"Frances Thorpe, special exhibitions, how can I help you?" The voice on the other end of the line was crisp and clear, with a hint of wariness. Something about it reminded Ashley of being sent to the principal's office as a kid. The Frances Thorpe who'd been making the rounds of every news show on the planet to talk about the controversy was calm, cool, and collected, her face a pleasant mask behind her wire-rimmed glasses. Untouchable, dapper, and fine, hot. The Frances Thorpe on the phone was bracing for a fight. God only knew the kinds of phone calls she'd been getting lately.

It took Ashley's scrambled brain a second too long to speak. "Hi Frances, this is Ashley Patterson." She flinched at the way her voice caught and then smoothed, putting on the most charming version of her accent. This was not a flirting call. This was business.

"Wait, what?"

Ashley plowed on. "Listen, I'm in the middle of a recording session, but I wanted to let you know I got your message. I will share the shit out of any fundraiser you set up." She bit her lip and inwardly cursed herself for cussing. The pause gave her an idea. One that would be far more cost-effective than trying to nail down a free venue. "But what if you sweetened the deal by offering rewards to donors?"

"What did you have in mind?"

"Donor tiers. Up to a certain dollar amount, it's a straight donation, or maybe they get a postcard and the exhibition booklet. But say, a couple hundred dollars and up gets you something in return."

"We don't have stuff to give away."

"Yeah, but I do. And I have friends who do. You have a party for the opening right? Charge double for the tickets and I'll play an acoustic set. You could give private after-hours tours of the exhibition. Stuff like that. People have raised serious cash for stuff like this by essentially auctioning off their time."

Silence. Ashley knew she wasn't crazy. But maybe museum people didn't do stuff like this. Maybe Frances Thorpe was so stuck in the grant-writing, corporate schmoozing cycle she couldn't think outside the box she was in.

"That's…I don't want to overstep my bounds, because I never knew them, but somehow that feels like exactly what Rian would have wanted. Guerrilla fundraising, damn the man."

And that was why Ashley wanted Frances Thorpe to have this. Got to feel it and smell it and get up close and intimate with Rian's work. She got it. "Rian would have been the first to admit that sucking the corporate teat was a necessary evil sometimes if you wanted to get real money, but yeah, they would have loved this. Fuck it, five grand gets you a print from my personal collection."

"I can't ask you to do that."

"You didn't. Look, I'm not saying I'm giving away my favorite print or anything. But if some rich asshole wants to drop five grand on a print and get to feel warm and fuzzy about supporting a small museum in the process? They can have one of my least favorites."

"I can do tours. The museum doesn't have much else we can offer."

"Trust me, we'll make it worth it to people. Let me make some phone calls. We'll get a donation page up and fill in the tiers with to-be-announced. You'd be surprised at what people are willing to give even before they know what the rewards are. We'll work out the details later."

"I don't know how to thank you."

"Don't thank me yet. Thank me when we pull this off. And we will, Frances, I swear to god we will."

"If we're going to work together, call me Frannie."

Oh god, Principal Frannie was even better than Principal Thorpe. Ashley squeezed her eyes shut. This was a professional relationship. They were working on a project together. Of course, she'd never been very good at keeping the personal and professional separate. See basically every relationship she'd ever been in, up to and including hooking up with Rian whenever one of them was lonely, bored, or horny.

Still, kicking herself didn't keep the flirtatious purr out of her voice when she responded, "Okay, Frannie." Nor did it stop the lick of satisfaction from warming her belly when Frannie audibly swallowed.

"And use my cell. God knows someone will post it online before too long, but for now, I know those calls aren't someone waiting to scream at me."

"I'm sorry."

"It's not your fault."

"I've had my fair share of bigots screaming at me. And sometimes I like pissing them off. But when it's not on your terms, it's exhausting."

PJ poked her head into the hallway. "We're ready for you, your highness."

She flipped off PJ. "Listen, I gotta go. Do you have some time tomorrow when we can iron out details?"

Chapter Three

F RANNIE MANAGED to hang up the phone before she let out the completely undignified squeal she'd been holding in from the moment Ashley's smoother than honey drawl climbed through the tinny speaker. Of course, as soon as she did, Holly came running into the room.

"What happened? Are you okay?"

"Ashley Patterson is about to rescue us, so yeah, I'm good."

"What? Really?"

"We're going to crowdfund it."

Holly cocked her head. "Ashley Patterson is going to rescue the show by crowdfunding it? I know we have a lot of eyes on us right now, but I don't know if that kind of straight fundraising is going to make up the difference."

Frannie sighed. Holly might be right, but it was worth a shot. They couldn't afford to lose the exhibition, in both actual ticket sales and the blow to her reputation. "It might not. But we're going to offer some incentives for big-money donors, and Ashley is going to play at the opening party, so we'll up the ticket price for that. Ashley is wrangling help from friends, and she's offering up a print in exchange for a five thousand dollar donation. We'll offer rewards with minimal costs, private tours and stuff like that."

"She's really going to give up one of Sampson's prints?"

"So she says. I'll believe it when I see it in writing. I wouldn't blame her if she came back and said her enthusiasm got the better of her."

"Still. Makes me wish I had five grand lying around." Holly came around to Frannie's side of the desk, watching over her shoulder as she set up an account with a nonprofit-friendly platform. "Have you mentioned this to the board yet? I don't think they're going to like it."

"I think if they want to keep the doors open they don't have a choice. Besides, if I do it and show money coming in, they really won't be able to say no. What are we going to do? Return donations?"

Once they had the site set up, Frannie chewed her lip. Of course the site immediately prompted the user to start sharing it on every social media platform known to man, but without board approval, she couldn't exactly send it to the museum's official accounts. Frannie had never been an "ask for forgiveness instead of permission" kind of person. She supported transgressive, progressive art and artists, but she was a rule follower herself. There was a reason she wrote grants and didn't make art.

She opened an email. Started typing. Deleted the words. She still couldn't believe she had any reason to be in possession of Ashley Patterson's email address. Maybe it was an elaborate prank. Their detractors would have to know how desperate Frannie would be. What if someone had called her impersonating Ashley offering help, and in reality she didn't give a shit about whether or not the show happened at this one little museum that would never get its hands on something like this ever again if she failed now.

Frannie pushed away from her desk and paced to the window. When this was all over, she could let the fear and anger and frustration that had been the undercurrent of every day since that greasy little weasel threatened her museum overwhelm her. She didn't have time for panic now, not with the straggling herd of protesters that had taken to camping across the street from the main entrance. Not with the future of the museum and the twenty years' worth of work she'd put in to get here in jeopardy.

Trenton Everett Markham III and his terrifying politics would not win. Not off her back, not on her watch. That bastard was going to rue the day he fucked with what was hers.

She sat back down, dashed out a few words and copied the link to Ashley. She might get fired for this stunt either way, but if it worked—when it worked—she would be able to leave with her head held high. She'd done everything she could to save this. For the museum. For the patrons who deserved access to this. For the kids who needed to see themselves. For herself.

With phones sent to voicemail and the museum buttoned up for the night, Frannie kept working through the evening. If her anger made her decide to put a near life-size portrait of a naked Ashley, all jet-black hair and heavy makeup, against a sunshine-yellow backdrop, standing straight-on, staring defiantly into the camera as the heat of the flash exposed every dimple, every stretch mark in the expanse of pale skin across her big belly and her wide hips, breasts hanging low— a visual "fuck you," if ever there was one— well, Frannie couldn't be blamed. They wanted to say it was pornographic, then she was going to meet them at the door with it.

· · ·

ASHLEY SAT up groggily with her alarm. Last night's session had been a series of frustrations punctuated by DMs to anyone she could think of with something to give to keep Frannie's museum afloat. Rian had always had a tight-knit group around them, but their straggling little family had suffered growing pains without Rian there to be the glue. They weren't dirty, sweaty kids at a basement show anymore. But they had a network, and she wasn't afraid to use it. Not for this.

She'd been distracted and unfocused, using up studio time they didn't have coming up with a plan to raise money for a museum she had no connection to other than she liked Frannie. Her passion for the project, her commitment to it, and hell, Ashley really liked the sound of her voice. And the dapper soft-butch thing she had going in interviews with her trim jackets and crisp white shirts and the slightly messy hair that Ashley wanted to run her fingers through. Not that she'd been tracking down clips of Frannie between takes. PJ had finally kicked her out at midnight to get some sleep and get her shit together.

Which she should be doing now. But first she checked the crowdfunding page. Money was trickling in at the lower tiers that promised a show postcard to the donor. Nothing for the big-ticket tiers, but they hadn't finalized what those would be yet. Ashley checked her messages. A new one from Frannie. This was business, she knew that, but her heart still went fluttery as she opened it. She did not have time for a crush right now.

You wouldn't happen to know anything about several large donations that came directly to the museum last night? I respect the rights of donors to remain anonymous, but if you had anything to do with it—and please tell me it wasn't you—I'd like to extend my thanks. They've likely spared me giving private tours seven days a week for the entire run of the show.

Ashley had her suspicions about who might have ponied up some real cash and wouldn't want to receive any kind of recognition or reward. She'd find a way to thank them later.

Lying on her bed, propped on her elbows, knees bent with her feet in the air like a damn teenager, she composed her reply.

It wasn't me, but I told you I was going to send some messages. I'll make sure to extend your thanks to the likely parties.

A thought, since you mentioned private tours. If the timing works for you, I could give a tour just prior to the opening. Their own personal trip down my memory lane in exchange for a sizable donation.

Let me know what you think. I'm home until about two and then I'll be in the studio and my bassist will actually kill me if we get any further behind schedule, so I'll probably have to surrender my phone. Just in case you were trying to reach me and couldn't.

She pressed send before she could rethink that last sentence. Despite the reputation for being a flirt that her drawling accent got her, she was terrible at it. And she wasn't supposed to be flirting with Frannie anyway.

She might live to regret offering to take a walk through the exhibition with a donor, just like she might regret offering to give up a piece of Rian's work. She joked about selling off her least favorite piece, but what she had in her possession was all too close, too real. She'd been holding on to them so tightly since the moment Rian's lawyer told her they were hers. The work was the only tangible thing Ashley had left of them.

There had been a time she'd been sure Rian was truly the great, if mostly platonic, love of her life. It was always going to be them, in the end. They both bounced between other lovers, other relationships, but Rian was it for her. And then Rian had stubbornly refused to do anything about their persistent cough—scared of the expense, yes, but more scared of going to a doctor as a person who didn't neatly tick a box of male or female—and then that cough had been the pneumonia that killed her best friend, the love of her life, her person.

Ashley had been lost. She'd spent the last eight years working herself into the ground to keep from feeling how much that loss hurt. She'd flirted and hooked up and scratched the occasional itch, but she couldn't fathom getting involved. It had taken her this long to attempt a career retrospective of Rian's work because she hadn't been able to bear looking at it until a year ago.

And then Frannie had walked into the proverbial room and Ashley was offering to give pieces of it away. To let strangers invade her memories. She set her phone on the nightstand. She would do what she'd said, she would help Frannie raise the money to keep the show, but that was it. If they weren't able to keep it, the work was going to sit in crates for eight weeks until the next stop because no one was going to be able to take it last-minute. Making this happen was in the best interest of the work. That was it.

"FRANCES, WHAT DID YOU DO?" Jonathan burst into her office without knocking and Frannie braced herself. If she was about to get fired, she wasn't going down without a fight. But first she had to get the trucking company delivering the work off the phone. The company she was now going to be able to actually pay, thanks to Ashley's anonymous friends.

When she had finished making the delivery arrangements, Frannie turned to her boss, still waiting in the doorway with his arms crossed. "I'm sorry, what?"

"Frances."

"You told me to handle it."

"And the museum appreciates receiving sizable donations

through its regular channels, especially ones specifically earmarked for this exhibition. But crowdfunding? What were you thinking? Do you even know what the tax implications are? The board is already shifty, they're going to be baying for your blood if we suddenly have the IRS breathing down our necks too."

"Which is why I specifically selected a platform that works with nonprofit fundraising. Think of it like an online silent auction. Everyone will get a tax statement, and anyone who wants to donate straight cash is being directed to the museum's website. It's no different than public radio offering tote bags in exchange for donating at a certain level. And yes, I talked to accounting and legal this morning."

"After you set it up."

"And we could have quietly taken it down if they'd given me a different answer. But we're losing time. The show delivers next week. We can't afford to do things through the usual channels. We should have had something like this up the minute the word boycott left that grease stain's mouth."

Jonathan shook his head. "On your head be it."

It was going to work. It had to. "I take full responsibility."

He left, and Frannie returned to her installation plans. The work was to be arranged in groupings, set by Sampson's team, each group mixing work from all stages of their career, emphasizing the narrative threads that carried through from their early experiments with the camera up until their death.

Ghostly black and white self-portraits from Sampson's freshman year of college showed their gradual shift toward androgyny from their assigned girlhood. The awkward angle of a cheap point-and-shoot selfie captured the relief and the tears on their face as their long hair was sheared away by a friend whose face was obscured by the heat of the automatic flash. Frannie remembered the feeling well, how cutting her hair boyishly short for the first time was liberating and terrifying, sitting in her desk chair in a dorm bathroom, watching a new outward identity take shape in the mirror.

All of those ugly beautiful feelings—the shaping of identity, the founding of a chosen family, the tangle of words for how it felt to not fit into the identity you were given at birth, the joy and defiance in creating a new narrative for people who looked like you, loved like you did, that wasn't a tragic cautionary tale, but a celebration and a middle finger— would carry the show from beginning to end. From Ashley's *fuck you* gaze in the first portrait, to the final grouping, which included a large family shot from Sampson's last Thanksgiving. A photograph dashed off without a thought, lovely regardless, but something more in retrospect, full of humor and tenderness, but with Sampson apart, behind the camera, watching the family they'd built from behind the lens.

Frannie was lost in the catalog, thinking about Sampson's own insistence that there was nothing precious or special about their work, to the point of stipulating that it be displayed unframed, using thumb tacks to affix it to the walls, when a list of promised donor rewards arrived from Ashley. She'd managed to go most of the day without squealing to herself about having Ashley in the museum, at the opening, giving a personal tour through the exhibition. Frannie hoped to hell she would be allowed to tag along for that. How differently must she see it, filtered through her memories of the events and of who Sampson had been, what they had been to each other. She was the Patti to their Robert, and even had the funding controversy to go with it.

The full list of offered incentives was impressive, and would even put them over-budget, which would mean offering free admission to more underserved kids. She couldn't assume they were going to get donors for every level. That would be foolish. But part of her still hoped.

. . .

Ashley,

This is more than I could have dreamed. This will break us even and then some if we can get donors at every level. There is some tax and legal stuff I'll have to send and have you forward to anyone else donating goods or time, and we'll need actual dollar amounts for everything to issue receipts.

Frannie paused, stuck for words to express her gratitude. She didn't understand why Ashley was so determined to make this happen for her little museum, why it felt like it was personal, and not just about making her friend's work accessible. It was in her head. It was personal to Frannie, so of course she would think it was personal to anyone else. Ashley probably didn't want to see the show sitting in storage for eight weeks if they couldn't make it happen here. That was all it was. Still, Frannie felt like she needed to say something more than thank you and talk about tax receipts.

I am stunned to the point of not having words for how grateful I am to have your support in this. It means so much to me to bring this exhibition into this community. I never want it to be as hard as it was for us to figure out who we were, but I never want to forget the work we did to make it easier for the next generation to be seen. Thank you for helping me fight for them.

She hit send before she could regret being overly personal.

Chapter Four

*U*s. She'd used the word *us*. Ashley had never been under the impression that Frannie Thorpe was precisely straight, but it wouldn't have been the first time she'd been fooled by a woman who erred on the side of short hair and trim suits for professional purposes. But she hadn't. And so her crush wasn't a ridiculous, certain to be unrequited one on a wholly unattainable straight woman. No, it was destined to be unrequited because this wasn't a personal relationship. And even if it wasn't professional, Ashley had only been keeping company with the hard ball of grief that sat in the pit of her stomach for the last eight years. There was too much distance, too much baggage, and too little time. She'd be back on the road the day after the show opened.

Her therapist would have things to say about it. More about running away from her grief, being afraid of connection. How new and different it was for Ashley to care enough about someone that she didn't want to scratch the itch that was Frannie with a one-night stand.

She was ethical. She never made promises she couldn't

keep. But she'd floated from brief connection to brief connection for purely physical release for years now. And it did its job. She mother-henned the people she loved—keeping them close to the point of smothering, if PJ had anything to say about it—and kept her distance from the people she fucked. She didn't mix the two. And someone like Frannie deserved more than that.

None of that stopped her from thinking about the other woman all damn day while she was in the studio. If Frannie's face was in her mind while she opened her mouth to sing, no one had to know. Just like she'd never admit how many times she'd been singing to Rian. The fact that anything could feel remotely similar, and over a woman she barely knew, should have shocked Ashley.

Maybe she was finally ready to move on. Maybe she was trying to justify getting Frannie into bed. But she'd never lied about who she was or what she wanted before and she wasn't going to start now.

She ran her fingers through her hair and pulled her pony-tail after her voice cracked, flubbing another take. Screaming until her voice broke was one thing when she'd been yelling at the top of her lungs in front of a loud as fuck two-piece punk band. She was trying to do something different now that she'd had the fear of vocal chord polyps keeping her from being able to sing at all put into her. She hadn't taken voice lessons for two years to have her voice crack on a take.

"What's with you, dude?" PJ asked from the other side of the glass as she scrubbed a hand over her face, dislodging the backwards hat that was keeping her long hair out of her face. "Is your throat sore or are you just not paying attention?"

The backing vocal tracks were literally the last thing on their schedule and she needed to nail them down and get it done and get the hell out of there. They couldn't afford additional time. It meant cramming a whole lot of vocal work into a short period of time, but she'd put it off to cobble together funding for Frannie and now she was stuck. She could not be distracted by a girl. She was not fourteen anymore. She was thirty-seven goddamn years old and she needed to get her shit together.

"It's nothing. Let's go again."

"I'm worried about you, Patterson."

PJ might complain about being mother-henned by Ashley, but she did the same damn thing. PJ had been the one to drag her out of bed, keep her going when she was too mired in depression to even remember to eat.

"I'm fine. Seriously." She spun her finger. "From the top."

EVERY DAY—A dozen times a day, if she was being honest—Frannie had checked the status of the fundraiser. The notifications of donor levels selling out and big-ticket items being snapped up had kept her phone buzzing at regular intervals, too. Why they hadn't considered this kind of effort from the beginning—well, she knew why. Their typical silent auction was a series of gift baskets from local shops and restaurant gift cards. They would never have been able to pull off something like this.

Ashley's pull even had regular donations rolling in. The development office was overwhelmed sending out new member thank yous and welcome packets. If they could retain even a fraction of them next year, they would be in the best financial shape in the museum's history. They could do so much good. Twenty years working almost entirely for nonprofits had taught Frannie to be cynical, but she couldn't stop a little spark of hope from clawing its way into her heart.

And it was all thanks to her. God, she needed to get a hold of herself before Ashley showed up for the opening. Between gratitude, admiration, and if she was being honest, the crush she'd been nursing for years that was only made worse by trading emails with her, Frannie was going to be tempted to throw herself at Ashley's feet and never leave. Add in her nerves about how Ashley would feel about the way they'd installed the show, the opening image, the way they'd laid out and juxtaposed the preset groupings to pull a particular narrative thread, and Frannie was probably going to be a puddle in a well-cut suit.

She had a few hours left to get her shit together before Ashley arrived to do a walk-through. She'd lead her personal tour immediately ahead of the opening tomorrow and the group would stay on for the official opening celebration.

Tomorrow, Frannie would be kept busy dealing with set-up and catering. And the police detail they'd had to request to keep Markham's rag-tag group of protesters from either harassing attendees, or worse, getting into the museum aiming to deface the work. Ashley had promised her that Rian would have been beyond tickled to have one of their photographs smeared with paint or eggs, but Frannie wasn't taking that risk.

Tomorrow night was going to be a goddamn triumph like the board had never dreamed of or seen. Whatever grumbling they had done about the controversy, the money, however many imaginary donors they thought she'd alienated by pushing for a contemporary-heavy schedule, she was going to have a museum full of people celebrating the work of Rian Sampson, with all of its identity politics on display.

Trenton Markham and his ilk could eat a bag of dicks. The news cycle was already moving on, and while his poll numbers still showed pockets of support, he wasn't going to win the primary. The exhibition's success, the amount of money they'd pulled in, was only going to be an embarrassment. His opponents were already using his failure to shut it down against him. Not that his challengers in the primary were much better, they all would rather people like her and Rian Sampson and Ashley Patterson go away—quiet or dead, it probably didn't much matter.

Her anger had carried her through the last few weeks, through load-in and installation, through pulling the threads of identity and confrontation in the work to make the show as visually challenging as possible. But Frannie was about ready to collapse. She was going to revel in her success and then hide in her office or her apartment between giving private tours.

She just had to get through the next forty-eight hours without embarrassing herself in front of Ashley or any of the museum members and guests. Easy. She'd done it a million times. But she hadn't done it when the special guest in question was a woman she'd been nursing a crush on, to whom she owed a massive personal and professional debt, and to whom she could never fully admit either of those things.

She'd be fine.

Holly knocked on the door frame. "Ashley's car just pulled up."

With her stomach tumbling nervously, like she was eighteen and asking out a girl for the first time all over again, Frannie stood, straightened her cuffs, pushed a stray bit of hair off her forehead, and went downstairs.

She could totally do this.

ASHLEY WAS STANDING in the lobby, hips swaying as she shifted her weight from foot to foot, when Frannie appeared from behind a door marked *Staff Only*. She was taller than Ashley had thought. That didn't help her nerves. She approached, hand outstretched, and Ashley felt like a hopelessly awkward teenager. She was supposed to be this badass rock star, and she was reduced to shyly taking this woman's hand, ducking her chin at Frannie's firm grip, and not wanting to let go.

The slight lift of the left side of her mouth as they each dropped their hands back to their sides was the kind of thing people wrote songs about. The kind of thing Ashley wrote songs about, the first verse that came before the heartache. *Get it together, Patterson.*

"Ashley, Ms. Patterson, welcome. We're so grateful you're here. But I expect you want to see the exhibition and get to your hotel for some rest."

"Please, it's just Ashley." Oh good, her accent was getting thicker. Because flirting with Frannie, in her place of work, was totally appropriate. "I'd love to see what you've done with it."

Frannie looked at the floor for a moment, flopping her dark hair forward in a move that shouldn't have been hot, but it was. Unbutton her shirt a bit, rumple her a little, and she would belong on a magazine cover. Ashley would have given anything to see what Rian would have done with a woman like Frannie.

"I hope…Well, I hope you're happy with the direction we've taken it in. Under the circumstances, with everything that's happened, I felt like we needed to make a particular statement, and…"

Ashley wrapped her hand around the other woman's wrist. "We wouldn't have approved you for the exhibition if we didn't trust you to install it in a way that honestly reflects the work. I know every curator is going to take it in a slightly different direction, editorialize it to suit whatever point they're trying to make. And I know you have a point to make. I trust you." Ashley let go and dropped her arm awkwardly to her side.

"I…Thank you." Frannie turned and bobbed her head in the direction of the far hallway. "It's this way."

Ashley followed her up a slight incline and to the left before she stopped short. She'd seen the image before, obviously, but seeing her naked body, with her stretch marks and her heavy tits, and the absolute *fuck you, I'm hot* on her face blown up almost bigger-than-life made her throat catch. She bit her lip and looked at herself, tough, defiant, secure. Rian had always made her feel like the most beautiful girl in the room. And goddammit, she was.

"Are you okay?"

"Yeah. I just…man, I remember that shoot. Rian was really into classical poses and themes at the time, but they wanted to make everything as bright as possible, make it impossible not to notice. Then we found that obnoxious yellow backdrop and I was originally going to keep my clothes on, but it was so hot under the lights that I said hell with it and got naked."

"You look so defiant. I may have been fueled by rage and caffeine when I chose that to open the show." Frannie grinned sheepishly and Ashley smiled back.

"It's a good choice. That asshole wants to say you're peddling porn, give him a naked fat girl that's so bright yellow you can't *not* look at it. Smart."

"It's just…It's a dare. You're daring the viewer to try to make you an object, and it won't work. You're a whole person. You know you're beautiful, but that's not all you are, and the rest of the world can shut up or fall in line. And god help anyone who looks at that and tries to insult you."

"Yeah, well, people did."

"People are assholes."

Chapter Five

I F A LARGE PART of Frannie's brain was engaged in
absolutely *freaking out* about the fact that she was getting
the secret history behind Rian Sampson's photographs from
the subject of so many of them, live, in person, in front of
her, and if that part was deeply confused if she was fangirling
more over Sampson or the woman standing in front of her,
well, who could blame her. Ashley was shorter than she'd
expected. Frannie had always assumed she was a tall woman,
given the size of her presence, but her short, chunky heels
barely brought her even with Frannie's shoulder.

Dammit, she was cute with her giant sunglasses pushed
up and holding her hair back. She was all sharp bangs, round
cheeks, and pointed chin, dressed down in a tunic and
leggings, face bare apart from a heavy coat of mascara and
berry lipstick. In person, the lilt of her southern accent was
stronger. Or maybe it was only that she was tired after a long
flight.

Frannie trailed behind her, letting Ashley move through
the exhibition at her own pace. She walked slowly, taking in
each grouping, moving between sets and walls without

saying much. Occasionally she lifted her hand to her lips, covering her mouth as she let out soft noises of recognition and, Frannie suspected, pain. It couldn't be easy reliving years of your life missing the person who'd left the document behind. She had so many questions, so many stories she wished she could know—how did that shot happen, where was this, how did you end up there, who were these people—but it wouldn't change anything to know and it wasn't her business.

They'd set up temporary walls both because they needed the extra space and to force traffic to flow in one direction through the gallery. When Ashley got to the final section before the exit doors, she sat hard on the floor and put her head in her hands.

"Are you okay?"

Ashley wiped her eyes and sniffed. "Yeah. It's…Fuck, it's a lot. I didn't think it was going to be this hard."

"You haven't been to any of the other openings?"

"Nope."

"I don't know if I should feel special or like a jerk."

She laughed weakly. "I'm glad I'm here, you know? I needed to do this. I've been avoiding it for years." She lay back on the floor and stared at the ceiling. "That Thanksgiving." She sniffed as another tear tracked across her temple into her hair. "God, I knew something was wrong. They'd been sick off and on, and that cough did not sound good. But I left the next day for London to be on a damn chat show and then back into the studio and doing promo and I knew I had this perfect, magical window to get so much shit done, to do and say all of these things and be loud and get heard and I couldn't give that up."

Frannie sat next to her, waiting for her to continue. She was tempted to take Ashley's hand, to offer some small comfort, reassurance, the way Ashley had done for her, but she let her hand fall awkwardly to the floor inches from the other woman.

"After, everyone wanted to talk about the failure of the healthcare system and the markets, and this was why we needed the ACA, to protect artists and freelancers who couldn't afford insurance the way it was before. And that was part of it, but Rian didn't give a fuck about the money. They would have found the money. They didn't go to the fucking doctor because going to the doctor for a cough when you're trans or nonbinary means spending half the time explaining to the doctor and the staff every detail of your gender identity and sexuality as if that has a thing to do with your goddamn pneumonia. And it's still like that. We still have these fucking people who want to be allowed to refuse to even see us, to have paramedics be allowed to let us die in the street if they think the way we live our lives is wrong. Rian didn't have a doctor they trusted, so they fucking died instead. And I am still so mad at them. But I'm more angry at people like Trenton goddamn Markham."

Frannie did clasp Ashley's hand then. "I know. God, I know. That's why…It's why I needed to do this. I grew up here. I didn't see people like me anywhere."

"Me either."

"Shit, at least I had Ellen and k.d. lang."

"Yeah, right? Like, yes, it got better, but in such a narrow way. And so slowly. It took me years to find queer femme role models." Ashley sat up and wiped her eyes, letting go of Frannie's hand.

"And it's not like I could tell people I wanted to look like k.d. lang when I grew up."

"You kinda do, though."

"It's the hair."

"It suits you." Ashley reached over and brushed an errant strand off Frannie's forehead.

"You want to get dinner?" Frannie blurted before she could let herself lean in and kiss her. She was not allowed to kiss Ashley Patterson, not in the museum, not while she'd just been crying over the memory of her last Thanksgiving with her dead best friend.

"I'd like that."

ASHLEY SPLASHED cold water on her face in the museum staff bathroom. Her eyes were still a little red, but she wasn't in terrible shape. She'd known it was going to be hard seeing Rian's whole body of work on display. She hadn't counted on how angry she would feel. They should fucking be here for this. They should be tagging along rolling their eyes at the idea of their work being worthy of a retrospective and wasn't the whole thing sort of gauche and hilarious, but hey, the champagne's free.

And Frannie. Jesus, Frannie. Sitting there while she raged and cried, just taking her hand and letting her do it. Someone like Frannie deserved so much more than someone like her and the one-night stands she had to offer.

She would have dinner with her, and go back to her hotel. She would paste a smile on her face and keep her shit together while she led a private tour through some of the most intimate, joyful, and painful moments of her life. Then she would get back on a plane the next morning and leave. Less than forty-eight hours to keep her hands to herself and not invite a woman to bed because she couldn't handle how much it still hurt.

Frannie was waiting when she emerged from the bathroom. "Any preferences? We don't have the widest variety of restaurants, but there's a decent sort of Mediterranean place nearby. It's a little pretentious, but the food's good."

"I'm sure it's fine. Variety where I come from means you have more than one fast food fried chicken place in town."

"We've got somewhat more variety than that. No good fried chicken, though."

She followed Frannie out of the building from a side entrance. "Careful coming around the corner. Most of the protesters are waiting for tomorrow, but there's been a determined little group all day and I'm pretty sure they've got things to throw."

"You shouldn't have to put up with this."

"The last month has taken years off my life, I'm sure. But we've presold more tickets than we thought we'd sell for the entire run, so I guess I can't complain?"

They slipped past a knot of people lurking across the street from the main entrance, their signs limp at their sides, condemning the queers and their pornography with snatches of poorly quoted scripture for good measure. The anger Ashley had felt in the room with Rian's work thrummed in her veins, rising to the surface. She'd never been very good at picking her battles and a screaming match with a homophobe might feel pretty good right about now.

"Don't let them have it. You know it doesn't do any good."

"It might make me feel better."

"So smack down some trolls on social media later. If you pick a fight with these people now, I have to order more cops here tomorrow, and I'd rather spend the money on giving museum passes to queer kids."

Ashley sighed. Frannie was right, of course, and she wouldn't pick a fight here. By the time she got back to her hotel room, she hopefully wouldn't want to pick fights with strangers on the internet either.

"I know. And you should. They need this more than I need to tell another bigot to fuck off."

"I mean, believe me, I get needing that. I've been tempted

more than once since this started to create a sock puppet account or twelve to knock down the people screaming at the museum online. Or the ones trying to publish my address or track down my parents and shame them for their lesbian daughter."

"Yeah, my mama's gotten some questions at church. But we got big before everyone and their grandma had social media, so we never got as much of that shit from strangers."

"I don't know if that makes it better or worse."

"You've never met my mother." Ashley grinned. "I got my chin and my temper straight from her. She can hold her own."

"Your family…" Frannie trailed off. She didn't need to finish the question.

"It was rough for a bit, not 'cause they didn't love me, but they needed time to wrap their brains around it, change the way they thought about my future. Rian's family wanted to bury them in a dress."

"Jesus."

"Yeah."

Frannie stopped in front of the door to a cozy-looking restaurant. "Look, if this is too much, if you need some time to decompress, I'll walk you back to your hotel."

"No. We should eat. I'm sorry I keep getting so heavy."

"Don't be sorry. I get it." Frannie held open the door for her to go in.

Ashley was quiet as the host led them to a table. Frannie wanted to change the subject to something lighter, but everything they had in common felt heavy. Rian, the exhibition, bigotry, the dismal state of healthcare for queer and trans people. Knowing now that Rian's birth family had rejected their identity added a whole other layer of meaning to the depth and strength of the family connections they'd forged as an adult. But all of that was too much for dinner. Too much to ask of Ashley, who Frannie barely knew, and who was doing her massive favor after massive favor.

Frannie kept quiet, waiting for a cue from Ashley as the other woman pulled a pair of sparkly, over-sized reading glasses from her bag and perched them on her nose.

"Don't laugh."

"Not laughing. Those are exactly the sort of glasses I'd expect you to have."

"I'm not always glittered up like a disco ball."

"Of course not. But you're generally a bit sparkly."

"I'm a magpie. When I was little, whenever I wandered off in a store, it was a good bet I was at the jewelry counter, or near the makeup, staring at the shiny things. I used to sleep with my favorite necklace under my pillow."

"I, on the other hand, was famous for running away in a mall when my mother and a saleswoman ambushed me with a frilly dress."

Ashley chuckled, a low, slightly scratchy sound in her throat that made Frannie's skin tingle. She wanted to hear it again. Their server interrupted to take their orders and allowed Frannie to change the subject away from the potentially thorny topic of childhood.

She asked instead about Ashley's work in the studio, her tour plans, the shift in her sound that she was working toward, distancing herself sonically from her old band as she got further into a solo career.

"Don't get me wrong, I love them to pieces and I love what we did, but everyone was ready to move on. We started when we were eighteen, playing basements and goofing off. We had stuff to say too, but we mostly assumed it would be this fun thing we did for a while, and it was, and we got way bigger than any of us thought we would, but we all knew we weren't going to do it forever."

"But you're still doing it."

"I can't stop. This is what I know how to do. Write songs, record them, do promo, go on tour, that's my life. Too much downtime and I get itchy."

All the more reason for Frannie to stop nursing this ridiculous crush. Ashley never stayed in one place for long. She would forever be in and out of town, running off to the next thing without stopping. Frannie's life was here. Her work, her family, she'd come back to her hometown for a reason. Turning the Briggs around to face the twenty-first century was an added bonus.

She shook her head. "That sounds like my nightmares. Never settling in, always living out of a suitcase."

"I'm disturbingly good at packing."

"I'd bet."

The conversation stalled, Frannie thinking about all the reasons she shouldn't be interested in the woman across from her. All the reasons she should get through the next day and let her go with thanks for everything she'd done for the museum. It wasn't about Frannie. It was about the work. But she couldn't shake the feeling of Ashley's hand wrapped around her wrist, telling her she trusted her with the installation. Or the way their fingers had twined together as Ashley lay on the gallery floor and cried for everything she had lost. No wonder the woman never stopped moving.

They skipped dessert and walked the few blocks to Ashley's hotel. Though the city technically spread across both sides of the river that split it, the downtown area was small. A small arena, a handful of hotels and restaurants, the museum, some shops, and a tiny park made up the whole of it. There was always talk of revitalizing the city, but no one ever wanted to spend the money to do it, so it languished as it was, not having changed much since Frannie was little.

She should have said goodnight in the lobby, but Frannie followed Ashley into the elevator. She was making sure she got to her room safely after a long day. Between traveling and the emotional upheaval of walking through the exhibition for the first time, she must be worn out.

Ashley slipped her key card into the lock. The door clicked. She opened it and flicked the light switch before she turned, holding the door open.

"Thanks for dinner." Ashley lifted onto her toes and rested a hand on Frannie's lapel, kissing her lightly on the cheek.

Frannie froze at the contact. If she turned her head just a hair, their lips would touch. If their lips touched, she would skim her hand from where Ashley's palm rested on her jacket, up her arm, to her shoulders, down the curve of her back, to her waist. She would pull her in and kiss her hard, back her into the room and let the door slam shut behind them. But that fantasy was best left for later, when the show was open and Ashley was gone.

"I should go."

Ashley was back on her flat feet, her hands at her sides. Frannie missed the warmth of her soft cheek, the weight of her palm against her collarbone.

"Good night, Frannie."

"Good night."

As soon as the door clicked shut, Frannie hurried down the hallway. She had to get out of this hotel before she changed her mind and knocked on Ashley's door.

Chapter Six

ASHLEY PACED the gallery opposite the exhibition. Frannie had told her last night that they'd moved what little of their collection was relevant into the space, but that it had been a struggle with their limited contemporary collection and the plethora of dusty still-lifes and donated seascapes by local artists. But they'd cobbled together a small grouping to ground the documentary narrative of Rian's work into a larger context.

That Frannie was really very good at her job did not make her less attractive. Nor did it help Ashley's conflicted feelings about the night before. She'd basically invited her into her hotel room. She'd kissed Frannie's sharp cheekbone and felt the racing of her heart under her lapel. And Frannie had left.

She'd hate it if she'd made Frannie uncomfortable. She'd regret knowing what Frannie's cheek felt like under her lips when she couldn't get it out of her head later, or stop herself from wondering if the rest of her skin was as soft and firm.

She'd told herself she was going to let Frannie go. It was for the best. She was leaving in the morning. There was no particular reason for her to ever see Frannie Thorpe again after tonight. Even if she wanted to.

"Wow." Frannie's voice at the door caught her off guard.

Ashley couldn't stop the grin from spreading over her face as she turned to the sight of Frannie looking her up and down. She'd dressed her part, in a tight silver sequined mini dress with cap sleeves that exposed her tattoos, black tights and sky-high heels that she'd inevitably ditch as soon as she started her short set. She sang better barefoot, always had, which led to some interesting scars on her feet back in the early days.

She blinked through her thick black lashes. Frannie was wearing a subtly-patterned charcoal suit, a pale lavender shirt, top button undone exposing her collarbone, a narrow, deep violet tie slung around her neck. "Wow, yourself."

Pink stained Frannie's cheeks as she tucked her hands in her pockets and scuffed her feet on the floor. "It's nothing. You look amazing."

"Never let it be said I don't give the people what they want." She'd crafted a signature look for herself years ago. Her tight stretchy dresses and refusal to hide her size or shape—as if a baggy dress would trick anyone into thinking she was thin—had started because it allowed her to move freely, but it had become a visual short-hand, a fuck you to an industry that wanted to whittle her down and fit her in a box.

"The donor group just arrived. If you're not ready, Holly can stall them for a few minutes."

Ashley took a deep breath, watching Frannie's fingers work to knot her tie. She'd walked through the exhibition again today, getting her bearings, picking and choosing what stories she would let go of and the memories she would keep for herself. She could hold those memories and turn them over without breaking down. Frannie was counting on her. She could do this.

"I'm ready."

THE CROWD BUZZED through the space, the steady hum of voices and clinking champagne glasses carrying Frannie through the evening. The opening was an unqualified success. Ashley's tour had been a pitch-perfect mix of funny insider stories and serious consideration of the work; the group that had ponied up the donation had gotten more than what they'd paid for. Even the stodgiest board members hovering at the edges of the room looked pleased, despite their sidelong glances at the very mixed group of their traditional patrons and the people who had bought tickets to the opening mostly for the novelty of seeing Ashley play an acoustic set in an art museum.

Frannie couldn't have imagined better. When they'd opened the doors tonight, she'd still been bracing for failure, but the protesters across the street hadn't deterred the ticket holders, nor had the added security measures of checking bags and jackets for any projectiles.

With a heady rush of adrenaline in her bloodstream, Frannie stepped up onto the small stage they'd erected for the night and tapped the microphone.

"Welcome, friends and patrons of the Briggs Museum of Art. For those of you who have been living under a rock and came out tonight only because you have annual tickets to museum events, I am Frances Thorpe, director of special exhibitions. For those of you who are here specifically because I accidentally embroiled the museum in a controversy over public arts funding, I would like to thank you, from the bottom of my heart, for being here with us tonight. Your support shows the museum, the community, and a nation watching at home, that the arts, no matter how challenging the material, have a place in public life that must be protected. We cannot shy away from work that asks us to consider lives different from our own. We cannot allow naked bigotry to silence the voices of artists like Rian Sampson."

Applause erupted and Frannie waved her arms to signal she wasn't done.

"This evening would not have been possible without the tireless support of Sampson's team, and in particular Ashley Patterson, who has so generously donated her time and effort in making our fundraiser a success. Ashley Patterson met Rian Sampson when she was eighteen, and their deep friendship and artistic collaboration will go down in history as one of the great partnerships between artist and muse. Patterson's own body of work, from music to model, and her activism in queer and body positive spaces, is its own powerful legacy, which she has been gracious enough to share with us tonight. Without further ado, friends of the Briggs, Ashley Patterson."

Ashley kicked off her shoes and adjusted the mic stand down to loud cheers from the half of the room that was clearly here to see her, and polite applause from the half of the room that was their regular patrons, slightly scandalized by either the noise or the barefoot woman in an art museum. What they would think of Ashley's set was anyone's guess.

"Y'all. Wow. It is super weird to be playing a set across from naked pictures of myself." Ashley grinned from behind the mic as the audience laughed. "I mean, I looked good, but still weird. But seriously, before I start, I wanna say thank you to all of you for coming out. Whatever brought you here, whatever compelled you to buy a ticket tonight, I hope you'll stand with us in fighting bullshit wherever you find it. This is for you, Rian. We are a long way from the basement, my friend. You should be here."

She turned her eyes to the ceiling, then slung a guitar over her shoulder and began to play a stripped-down version of one of her old fight songs, her big voice flooding the space. She held the room, winding a spell around every single person. Every time she closed her eyes on a long note, the audience held their breath. Every time she opened them again, everyone thought she was looking directly at them.

But as she transitioned into a song Frannie hadn't heard before, she was pretty sure Ashley really was looking at her, catching her gaze through a song that was both sad and lovely, drawing more on blues and vintage country than punk. It was a song about constant motion, never waking up in the same place more than a few days in a row, with a wailing, lilting chorus, punctuated by her voice dropping softly, just barely breaking. Frannie's chest hurt for her, thinking of how long Ashley had been running from the loss.

"Thanks y'all. That one was new," she murmured to the applause before she launched into another older song, letting the audience sing along for the chorus, dispelling the melancholy for a giddy burst of adrenaline and joy. Frannie nodded at the approving looks of the board members and let the energy of it carry her away, leaving behind Frances Thorpe, special exhibitions director to just be Frannie, watching Ashley Patterson dance around barefoot with a guitar and lead a room in the chorus of a song about making out with girls in clubs. They had pulled it off.

Chapter Seven

A SHLEY WAS SURPRISED at how buoyant the energy was. It had been a long time since she'd played to such a small room, and worse, one where she could see every face in the crowd reacting. But they were into it. She'd even caught some of the old farts from the board nodding their heads. And Frannie.

Frannie's gaze on her was almost enough to break her. Every time Ashley glanced in her direction, she noticed a subtle shift in her posture as Frannie realized they'd done it. The opening was a rousing success and the exhibition would make money. They would have their pick of sponsors who actually supported the arts, and not just the art that was politically safe and boring. Frannie had put them on the map.

By the time she stepped off the makeshift stage, Ashley was sweating and floating on a wave of relief and adrenaline. She beelined to Frannie and threw her arms around her waist, just barely stopping short of kissing her. Frannie's arms came around her shoulders and they swayed in place as they both spoke at once.

"You were amazing!"

"We did it, we did it, we did it!"

Frannie laughed, the sound of it singing through Ashley's body, making her shiver despite the warmth of the room and the flush from performing. They parted, though Frannie took her hand.

"I couldn't—I don't know how I'll ever thank you enough. I couldn't have done this without you."

"You would have thought of something. But I'm glad you came to me."

Ashley was forced to let go by a stream of people wanting to congratulate both her and Frannie. By the time the caterers cut off the wine and the crowd started to thin, Ashley's voice was raw from talking over the noise and she'd lost count of the number of hugs she'd given.

Frannie's assistant shooed them out the door with a "go celebrate" and a raised eyebrow.

Frannie's cheeks colored. "You must be exhausted."

"Wide awake, actually. But you could still walk me back to my hotel." If Frannie wanted to pretend that was an innocent remark, if she wasn't interested, Ashley would let her. If not, if she wanted to come back to Ashley's room…

Frannie interrupted her thought. "If you're ready to get out of here…"

Ashley took Frannie's hand and squeezed. If she could keep contact with her, maybe neither of them would lose their nerve.

At the door to her room, Ashley dropped Frannie's hand to fumble through her purse for the key. Frannie stood behind her, her front to Ashley's back, the length of her frame dwarfing Ashley, the width of Ashley's hips and belly spreading past Frannie's bounds in the gray shadow they cast on the door. Frannie was warm behind her, bundled in her neatly-cut suit as Ashley's skin cooled away from the crowded gallery and coming down from the high of their success. Exhaustion was starting to creep into her limbs, but Frannie's lips brushed the back of her neck as the lock clicked, sparking a fire low in her belly. No matter how tired she was, she would stay up for this.

She'd thought they would paw at each other, roughly shucking clothes in a frantic race to the bed, running on post-show adrenaline, but Frannie resisted Ashley's instinct to rush. Backed against the wall inside the door, Frannie leaned over her and took her mouth, traced her lips delicately, as if they had all the time in the world to learn each other.

Ashley tangled her fingers in the soft, short hair at Frannie's nape, kissing her back, pressing her body against Frannie, finding her softer than she'd expected. Everything about this woman was a surprise.

But they couldn't stay by the door kissing all night. There wasn't time.

Ashley took Frannie's hand and led them to the bed. How many cheap hotel coverlets had she pressed her naked back against over the years? She pushed the thought away. She wanted this. Needed this. Wanted Frannie, here, now, for however long she could stay awake before she had to leave for the airport.

When her knees hit the mattress, she stopped and shimmied her dress down over her shoulders. Frannie swallowed hard as Ashley peeled the fabric down her body, exposing her chest and her belly, until with a swing of her hips, she dropped the dress to the floor and stood in her underwear.

Frannie stood there, watching her, not moving. "Come on, you've seen naked pictures of me." Ashley fidgeted, tilting her hip with her weight on the outside of one foot, suddenly nervous.

"Not the same thing. Not the same thing at all." Frannie reached out and skimmed her fingers up Ashley's arm, across her collarbone, down to the crease of her cleavage. She traced her thumb across the smooth fabric of Ashley's plain, practical bra, following the deep curve of her breast as she leaned in and pressed her mouth to the corner of Ashley's jaw. "I suppose this is as good a time as any to admit that I've had a crush on you for years."

With Frannie's teeth on her neck, Ashley's brain got stuck between surprised laughter and melting arousal and she huffed out a strangled noise. "You know, I told myself I was watching all your interviews because I needed to know what was going on with the show, but really, I just thought you were super hot."

Frannie let out a startled laugh and froze with her fingers tracing Ashley's bra strap. "You did?"

"I did." Ashley sat and pulled Frannie's hand until the other woman sat beside her. "Can I touch you?"

"Yes."

She slipped her hands around the column of Frannie's neck, framing her jaw with her thumbs, stroking her soft skin before she leaned over for another kiss. "Can I take off your jacket?"

"Yes."

Ashley trailed her hands across Frannie's shoulders, over the soft satin lapels, and slipped her fingers under the fabric, following her collarbone to slide the jacket from her shoulders. She lifted each of Frannie's hands out of the sleeves and left her sitting on the end of the bed, leaning back on her hands, as she took it to the closet and carefully hung it up.

Frannie's chest rose and fell rapidly under the fine cotton shirt, her breasts straining the buttons slightly on each deep inhale, her tie askew. Ashley wanted her naked, to taste her skin, to feel the hidden curve of her hip under her palm, the softness waiting at the center of her. But Frannie deserved better than a quick fuck and Ashley sensed she needed it.

She stepped in front of her, framing Frannie's legs between her own. "We can stop anytime."

"Don't stop."

"Can I take off your tie?"

Every piece of clothing she peeled away from Frannie revealed something new. Freckles dotted her shoulders. Her nipples were deep brownish pink and sensitive to the slightest touch. Her hips softly padded, her belly slightly round, every permission she granted Ashley was like a new piece of the treasure map that was Frannie's body.

"I want to touch you." Frannie was down to her black briefs, sprawled on her back on the coverlet while Ashley straddled her hips, tonguing her nipples into sharp peaks while Frannie huffed and moaned under her.

"You can touch me."

Frannie tangled her fingers in Ashley's hair, pulling slightly as Ashley ran her teeth across her ribs. Her free hand skittered across Ashley's shoulder, pushing her slightly to the side.

"Do you want me to stop?"

"No. Yes. I want…" She patted the bed next to her. With her disheveled hair, blown pupils, and Ashley's slight teeth marks on her skin, Frannie looked completely undone. Debauched, even. Her normally buttoned-up, articulate self lost in a haze of arousal. Ashley would give her whatever she wanted.

She lay next to her. Frannie rolled to her side and kissed her, harder than before, as her hand skated over the plain, sturdy fabric of Ashley's bra, like she was trying to work up the courage to really touch her. Ashley stopped her hand and placed it firmly over her breast.

"You can touch me. I want you to."

Frannie kissed her and stroked her thumb over Ashley's nipple, the sensation dulled by the heavy fabric. She reached behind her back and unhooked it, wriggling away to strip out of it before pressing their bodies back together, threading her leg between Frannie's.

"Is this okay?" She rolled her hips against Frannie's firm thigh, a spark of pleasure rising up her spine from the pressure.

"Yes." Frannie's hips twitched in response. "God, yes."

They twined together, kissing stroking, touching, hips working against thighs in a stuttering rhythm until they were both out of breath. Frannie slowly grew bolder, her fingers working Ashley's nipples as they writhed, sliding down her spine to cup her ass, fingers digging into soft flesh, pulling Ashley's body against her thigh.

Frannie was hot against her skin, her underwear damp where their bodies met. Ashley's body answered with its own heat, her own slickness soaking through her panties as her body clenched and stuttered against the building pressure, pleasure buzzing in her belly, in her breasts where Frannie's fingers stroked and squeezed, in the curve of her ass as she guided the movement of their hips, on her lips and tongue, her neck and the sweet spot just below her earlobe as Frannie's teeth ghosted over her skin.

The sound of their shared breath filled the room; pants and gasps of pleasure traded between them until the fire in Ashley's body crested, swelling and rolling over her skin as she tensed and tipped her head back to moan out loud. Frannie's teeth caught her throat as she stuttered against Ashley's body with a low gasp, her grip on Ashley's hip clenching as she ground against her and slowed to a stop.

She bowed her body against Ashley, the hair at the crown of her head tickling Ashley's chin. Ashley carded her fingers through Frannie's hair and in a fit of tenderness kissed the top of her head. Leaving this town, this room, this woman, was going to be so much harder than she'd bargained for.

. . .

Frannie would have sworn she was dreaming. It couldn't be possible that she was lying in bed with Ashley with her head buried in her neck while Ashley stroked her hair. She was sweaty and mostly naked and she'd just come against Ashley's thigh.

"Am I dreaming?"

Ashley's chest shook under her head as a burst of bright laughter broke the spell. "No, baby." She petted Frannie's head again.

Dear god, she had less than zero game or chill. But at least she could stick her face in Ashley's naked chest in her shame. "Sorry."

Ashley laughed again, the sound filling the small room. "I don't think anyone's going to be able to top that as a post-sex compliment."

Right. Other lovers. Ashley was leaving in the morning. She'd never see her again. Once the show left the museum and all the donor prizes had been fulfilled, there wouldn't be a reason for them to ever talk again. Frannie sat up and reached for her undershirt.

Ashley grabbed her wrist. "I'm starving. You want room service?"

Delaying the inevitable by sharing a meal half-naked in bed was a terrible idea. But she was hungry, it was late, and while drawing out their parting with another small intimacy was going to hurt later, Frannie couldn't say no. She'd stay as long as Ashley let her.

"Sure."

They ended up splitting a waffle sundae, leaning against the headboard, the tray perched on their legs as they traded bites, Ashley wrapped in a robe and Frannie in her undershirt. Ashley had showered while they waited, and the sight of her warm and damp, bare-faced, wrapped in a towel would be burned into Frannie's brain forever.

"This is totally what I thought staying in hotels was always like when I was a kid." Ashley dipped her finger in the melted ice cream and hot fudge on the empty plate.

Frannie reached and pulled her sticky-sweet fingertip into her mouth. Ashley bit her lip and blinked heavily. They'd talked too much. Frannie couldn't let herself forget what this was, that they weren't lovers, they weren't even friends. She'd crashed into Ashley's world with a plea for help and now that the work was done, Ashley would go back to her real life.

She picked up the tray and set it on the dresser before she pulled Ashley down and licked hot fudge from the corner of her mouth. A few more stolen hours. One more time.

Just before dawn, Frannie carefully slid out of bed as Ashley slept. She gathered her clothes, half-dressed, and sat at the desk with the hotel pen and paper. She didn't want to be there to say goodbye, but she couldn't leave without saying anything. She wrote, expressing her gratitude again, saying she understood that there was no reason for them to see each other again, but Ashley could always find her if she wanted. She folded the paper and slipped it in her pocket, finally settling on the words she left behind.

Ashley,
Thank you for a perfect night.
Frannie

Chapter Eight

ASHLEY WOKE to the shrill sound of the hotel phone, bleating out her wakeup call. She fumbled to pick up the receiver and set it back down with a clatter. She had to haul ass to gather her things and get herself to the airport, but she would be happy to linger in bed for another minute with Frannie. Who wasn't there.

The other side of the bed was cold. Ashley sat up and rubbed at her eyes. Frannie was gone.

It shouldn't have bothered her. Under normal circumstances, it would make life easier, to not have an awkward morning-after *we both know this was just a one-time thing, right* conversation. But after last night, after sex and waffles and more sex, she'd wanted to say goodbye. To make foolish promises about staying in touch and seeing each other again whenever Ashley was in the area. It was probably better that Frannie had left.

She peeled herself out from under the covers and picked up her discarded dress from the foot of the bed. Her bra had landed somewhere near the desk, where she saw the note.

Simple words in Frannie's clear, firm handwriting. It had been a perfect night.

A perfect night that haunted her from the hotel to the airport, through green rooms and post-show parties and politely turning down people she might otherwise have made out with on late-night dance floors.

If it had only been the sex, maybe she would have gotten over it. She could have gotten it out of her system with someone else, some other woman she barely knew. But she couldn't shake the feel of Frannie's hand in hers, her back on the floor of the gallery, tears leaking into the hair at her temples while she grieved for Rian all over again. Frannie's quiet support, her tacit understanding that some losses you never get over, you can only learn to live with, followed her across Europe like a ghost.

PJ caught up to her, scrolling through photos she'd taken on tour, wishing she could tell their stories to Frannie, getting half-way to starting an email or a text and stopping herself. That note had been Frannie's final goodbye. *Thank you for a perfect night* didn't exactly invite her to continue the not-relationship. They'd done what they set out to do and it was over.

But for the first time in years—for the first time since Rian —Ashley wanted more. She wanted late-night phone calls from crappy hotel rooms and screwing up time zones but not caring because she got to talk to her person for five minutes before she fell asleep. She wanted a person. She wanted long hugs at baggage carousels and hot reunion sex and lazy makeouts at home. And she wanted it with Frannie, with all her buttoned-up passion and nerdy enthusiasm. She'd eat waffle sundaes and talk about art and music and politics with her forever.

"Would you just talk to her already?" PJ flipped a chair around and straddled it, long dark hair tucked under a backwards baseball hat, and stared meaningfully at Frannie's phone.

"What?"

"Dude. How long have we been friends? You have been mooning over that woman for weeks."

Ashley looked up at the ceiling and sighed. "I know."

She glanced at her makeup kit, spread out on the counter. She should have been getting geared up to go on stage, to run around and sing her heart out and put on a show. But she was fucking exhausted. She wanted to go home. And she wanted to go home to someone.

"So talk to her already."

"It's too late."

"Ash, I'm saying this because I love you. Rian is gone. Rian has been gone. And they would be so fucking mad at you for moping around after them. Live your fucking life, dude. Go get the girl."

PJ's words hit her hard. They'd had this conversation before. It was nothing new. Rian would be mad at her for carrying around a grief-laden torch for so long. She could practically hear their voice in her head telling her to move the fuck on.

"I don't know how."

PJ shifted in her chair and grinned. "I might have an idea."

FRANNIE PACED THE GREEN ROOM, wearing a track in the carpet from the couch to the snack table to the bucket of mini water bottles and back to the couch, fingering the folds of the speech in her trouser pocket, rehearsing her words.

When she'd gotten the call that she was being recognized for her work on the Sampson exhibition in the face of protest, and for the success of the fundraising efforts that allowed the museum to expand its outreach to queer teenagers, Frannie had been shocked. By the time it came, months later, when the show had moved on to another city, when she'd almost stopped waking up every morning with the ghost of Ashley's skin under her fingertips, when Trenton Everett Markham III had been thoroughly trounced in the primary, not even making it to the general, she had nearly forgotten just how many talk shows she'd been on, how much national attention it had gotten.

The whole thing was a blur in her memory until Ashley showed up. No matter how much she wished those memories would fade like the others, every moment she'd spent with Ashley in those two days was as sharp and bright as if it had been yesterday.

Writing her speech hadn't helped. She couldn't talk about the show, the fundraising, the free tickets they'd been able to give to gay-straight alliances from all over the state—none of it would have been possible without Ashley. And Frannie couldn't think about Ashley without thinking about that night, and the note she'd left behind when she slipped out in the bruised light before dawn.

She'd known when she went back to her room that it wasn't meant to last. It was a one-time thing, fueled by the adrenaline of success. Frannie had wanted to leave it at that, keep it clean and neat. She didn't need Ashley to know that she would be holding that one perfect night in her sense memory every morning when she woke up alone.

But now she was here, and a PA was ushering her to the wings, and she had a speech to give, thanks and acknowledgment to make to Ashley, who was somewhere in Europe based on Frannie's masochistic social media stalking.

Except Ashley was there, on stage, behind the podium, in a surprisingly understated red sheath dress. Frannie's hearing fuzzed out. Ashley beckoned her with an arm raised to her side of the stage, her grin wide. A hand at her back pushed Frannie out of the wings and into the light.

Ashley took Frannie's elbows in her hands and kissed her cheeks, her sky-high heels bringing her up to Frannie's height.

"What are you doing here?" Frannie resisted the urge to pull Ashley into her arms.

"Later." Ashley squeezed her elbow. "You have a speech to give."

Shaken, Frannie stepped up to the podium, pulled her speech from her pocket, and inhaled, looking out at the sea of dim faces on the other side of the stage lights.

"Well this is…unexpected." The audience chuckled. "I was going to tell you all about how I really don't deserve this recognition because Ashley Patterson was the reason we were able to raise the money and fund the exhibition after our largest corporate sponsor dropped us, but now she's here."

Frannie turned to see Ashley behind her, laughing and blushing slightly, before she yelled loud enough for the microphone to pick it up, "You deserve it and more, darlin'."

Frannie's cheeks warmed, and she stared at the creased paper in front of her. Giving her speech was going to be one of those things she would only remember if someone showed her a recording of it. Her brain was too focused on Ashley's presence behind her to form a memory of thanking the board for not firing her, the museum's supporters for buying tickets and making it the most attended special exhibition in the museum's history. She wouldn't remember thanking people for sending a giant middle finger to people who wanted to undo the progress their community had made, or acknowledging the work they had left to do.

Her memory would only pick up again when she left the

stage, and between the layers of curtains, Ashley took her hand.

"What are you—"

Ashley put two fingers over Frannie's lips. "Later. Now all I wanna know is if I can kiss you."

Frannie didn't answer, she dipped her knees, cupped Ashley's jaw in her hands, and brought their lips together. Past and present tense collided, the press of Ashley's mouth familiar and new, her fingers tangling in the hair at Frannie's nape somehow right, the thing she'd been dreaming about for months real again, imprinting on her brain.

"How are you real?" She whispered with her forehead resting on Ashley's. "How are you here?"

"I want to stop running away. Or run away with you. I'm not sure. But I think it has to be with you."

"Why now?"

"I can't stop thinking about you. And I don't want to. I want to tell you things and know how you are, and I want to spend the night with you all the time. I haven't felt like this about anyone in a long time, and it scares me. I lost the last person I wanted to love this much."

"I know." Frannie ran her thumbs over the swell of Ashley's round cheeks, dusted with blush and powder, and kissed her forehead. "But my life is here, and your life is out there."

"It is. Some of the time. But I'm so fucking tired, Frannie. I just want to come home."

"And you want home to be with me?"

"I want to try. If you'll have me."

"Of course I'll have you."

Frannie folded Ashley into her arms, Ashley's head resting on her collarbone, and nothing had ever felt more like home.

Author's Note

Frannie and Ashley's story takes a huge chunk of inspiration from the funding scandals the National Endowment for the Arts found themselves embroiled in, starting in 1989 with exhibitions by Andres Serrano and Robert Mapplethorpe, among others. Slashing public funding for the arts has been a conservative line-item favorite ever since, despite its already meager percentage of any budget.

While the surrounding circumstances of the story draw heavily from the episodes the kicked off the "Culture Wars," Rian's own work is inspired mostly by artists working in the late nineties and early aughts who were documenting queer and youth cultures. In my head Rian's work is a mash-up of the portraits of Catherine Opie and the documentary-style work of artists like Wolfgang Tillmans and Ryan McGinley. Throw in a dash of Nan Goldin, a smattering of Francesca Woodman, and you have something like Rian's style.

Queer and other marginalized people have always been making art, the magic of the internet is that it is easier than ever to support them. Whether you sign up for someone's

Patreon, Kickstarter, purchase from sellers on Etsy, or check out hashtags like #showupforwishes or #transcrowdfund, I hope this story inspires you to support marginalized creators in whatever way you can.

62

Also by Sionna Fox

Bondage in Boston

Bound To

Tied Up

Short Stories and Novellas

"Fight Fire with Fire"

Dark Rooms

"Etudes"

Wolf Summer

Standalone

Satisfaction

BONDAGE IN BOSTON BOOK ONE

Bound to

SIONNA FOX

Chapter One

Goddammit, Izzy. I pressed the button on the side of my phone, checking the time. Again.

It was times like these I missed smoking—standing outside a bar, waiting for my best friend in the sticky August-in-Boston heat. Smoking gave you something to do with your hands and a weird solidarity with the other smokers hovering in doorways, sweating or freezing, depending on the season. Instead, I fidgeted and made repeated vain attempts to unplaster my hair from the back of my neck.

Though the sun had finally set on another day of the New England trifecta—hazy, hot, and humid—radiant heat still billowed up from the pavement, keeping the temperature in the city on this side of stifling. I wanted a cigarette. I wanted to be at home in Vermont where I could jump in the pond or float down the river to cool off. I wanted to be where there weren't miles upon miles of pavement, glass, and brick exhaling their heat all night. The whole city was sticky, sweaty, and irritable.

If I couldn't submerge myself, I at least wanted to be at

our apartment, parked in front of the fan with a drink, not waiting for Izzy outside of a bar that wasn't really a dive bar so much as a *we'll overcharge for cheap beer for irony's sake* bar. If I was going to drink crappy beer for irony's sake, I didn't want to pay a hipster surcharge for it.

My phone buzzed in my hand and I nearly dropped it in my rush to read the message.

Izzy: Sorry! Running late! Be there in ten!

Isolde Roth had been my best friend since we were thrown together freshman year of college by the forces of fate or the untold wisdom of the housing office. After a decade of friendship, you would think I'd have learned never to show up on time for a date with Izzy, let alone early, but I was constitutionally incapable of being late. I was raised by people who punched clocks. Habitual lateness meant losing your job, which would set off a downward spiral of ever-worsening consequences, finally landing somewhere in a gutter. My parents may have exaggerated a bit, but the lesson stuck all the same. Clock-watching bosses loved me.

Knowing in Izzy's world "be there in ten" could easily mean fifteen, twenty, or worse, I opted to suck it up and brazen it out at the bar, hoping to get a whiff of air conditioning. I grabbed a stool where I could see the door to wave Izzy over to my rescue the second she walked in. I ordered a bourbon—rocks, in a nod to the weather—and did my best not to play with my phone. It was a losing battle. I fidgeted and checked the door every five seconds while my hands got clammy. Even though I knew she was coming, eventually, the mean girl in my head whispered that I was being abandoned, that I had finally driven my best friend away, how sad and pathetic I must look, twenty-eight and alone on a Friday night, all dressed up with no friends. Once Izzy showed up, I would be fine, but sitting by myself, surrounded by strangers, triggered my anxiety, making my breath come short and my hands sweat.

My neck was starting to ache from all the head-swinging to watch the door when not Izzy, but a tall man walked into the room. He was long and lean, broad at the shoulder tapering to a narrow waist. He was built like a runner, and I imagined the view from the rear must be fantastic. He stepped forward, and I was like a deer in headlights, holding my breath and staring. Dark, slightly shaggy hair hung over his forehead, obscuring his eyes until he lifted a long, elegant hand to push the locks away. Something about him made me think he could toss a girl around a bed like a rag doll. Which suddenly sounded like an excellent way to spend a Friday night.

He scanned the room and his gaze caught mine. Busted. I was blatantly ogling the guy. Heat crept up my cheeks, but I didn't want to lose our spontaneous staring contest. God, he was pretty. From where I sat, his eyes looked to be the same deep brown as his hair. The corners crinkled slightly when he lifted one side of his full mouth, like it was the least surprising thing in the world to have women stare at him. Cocky bastard. I scored a minor victory when a clap on the shoulder from another guy forced him to break his stare as his friend led him away to the far corner of the bar.

Holy shit. I let out a long breath, took a slightly-too-large swig of my drink, and nearly choked as the liquid burned down my throat to pool in my belly. The choking distracted me long enough to miss that not only had he approached the bar to order, but he was standing next to me. I stared resolutely at the dark, polished wood in front of me as he ordered a beer. He took the stool next to mine while he waited. I could feel his gaze on me, but I was completely and utterly frozen, trying to talk myself through the process of breathing in and out before I fainted.

"Hi," he said, a hair too near to me, in a low voice that made a simple greeting sound provocative and dirty, like he could boss me around and I'd enjoy every second of it. I shivered. That image and his voice were going to be burned into my brain.

"Hi," I croaked, chancing a look up at his face.

Oh, he got better up close. His eyes were a few shades lighter than his hair, his jaw firm and dusted with a five o'clock shadow, a slightly crooked nose because no one is that perfect. And his mouth. I wanted to nibble on his full lower lip like it was my job. Obviously, I resumed staring at the bar in paralyzed silence until the bartender delivered his beer. He paid and left without saying another word to me. I snuck a peek as he turned a corner and disappeared. I was right about the view. I might have even whimpered. A little. Or a lot, considering the quizzical look from the bartender as he collected the tip his unholy hotness had left behind.

If Izzy didn't show up soon, I was going to explode. I felt like the world's biggest dork, clamming up like a twelve-year-old with her first crush over a guy in a bar. *A guy, Jo. A human man. A fucking gorgeous human man, but still human.* He must have some epic flaws to be that pretty. It was a trade-off. It had to be, or the universe was even more of an asshole than I already thought.

Izzy must have floated in while I was talking myself out of a panic attack. "Hello, Earth to Jolene," she said, shaking my shoulder gently.

"*OhthankGodyou'rehere.*" I almost launched myself into her lap.

"Whoa, there, lady. I'm not that late." She glanced at her phone. "Okay, fine, I'm pretty late, but what happened?"

"Just… Fuck, I wish I wasn't so awkward. I got caught staring at this stupidly hot guy, then he actually spoke to me, and I kind of maybe completely lost the ability to form words," I blurted and hung my head in my hands, another wave of embarrassment roiling in my guts in the retelling.

"What? Where is this guy?" She sat up and craned her neck, peering into the bar's dimly lit corners.

"Does it even matter? I'll never see him again. We can never come back to this bar. I should probably go back to our place and start collecting stray cats."

"Oh, sweetie, we're not allowed to have cats in our apartment. And you've been in Boston for a week." She rubbed my shoulders and I relaxed in increments. "You can't give up yet, my little Country Mouse."

"I know. I'm tired and overwhelmed. I'll be fine. Totally not about to pack up the car and run for home. At all. Nope."

"You will do no such thing, Jolene Mae Whitman," she ordered in a passable imitation of my formidable Nana.

"Yes, ma'am."

"Damn right, yes, ma'am. Buck up, camper. Come on, this is our first night out in our new town. If you're not going to talk to him, we can at least look."

"No, we can't. Because you'll find some reason to go talk to him, drag him over to our table, and it will be Friday nights in Canfield all over again, with you trying to set me up with people, and no, thank you."

"That was *one time*."

"Dude, that was every weekend."

"Whatever. Fine. Be that way." She raised her beer. "Cheers to us, and especially to you, Country Mouse."

I clinked my glass with hers and gave her my brightest, bravest smile. "Cheers to us." I drained my drink and plunked it on the bar with a satisfying thump right as Izzy's eyes lit up.

"No. Fucking. Way." She hopped off her stool. "Wait here."

I spun in my seat and watched her weave through the crowd of finance bros and grad students, toward the far corner. My stomach made a mad dash for my throat. *No. Nononononononono. This is not happening.*

She came back with Tall, Dark, and Gorgeous in tow, chattering animatedly.

"This is so weird. Do you live around here?"

"No, I'm closer to the hospital. You just moved in, right?"

"Yeah, I start my MFA after Labor Day." She turned to me. "Jolene, this is Molly's brother, Matt. Matt, Jolene."

He held out his hand. I took it, and his warm fingers engulfed mine. "Nice to meet you."

I mumbled something in return and ducked my gaze at the sharp, electric thrill that ran through me at his touch. I dropped his hand before it got weird that I didn't want to let go. A burning need to know what his large hands would feel like everywhere warred with the impulse to run away as quickly as possible. Deer in headlights must have done it for him. He looked at me appraisingly, something like curiosity in the slight narrowing of his eyes.

He glanced over his shoulder, breaking the spell, letting me take a deep gulp of air now that his gaze wasn't fixed on me.

"I should get back. It's good to see you, Izzy." He turned to me. "Nice to meet you again, Jolene."

"Yeah," I managed with a smile that probably looked more like a nervous grimace. He and Izzy stepped away as they exchanged numbers, promising to hang out sometime. I knew she'd known him since forever, but I hated how easy it was for her, how much I was always Izzy's awkward side-kick. I picked a spot of chipped varnish in front of me.

As soon as he walked away, Izzy turned to me, eyebrows scrunched in concern. "Are you okay?"

I balled my fists and shook my head. "So that guy I choked in front of earlier? The one I didn't want you drag-ging back to our table?"

She covered her mouth with her hands. "Oh my god, that was Matt?"

I nodded.

Izzy bit her lip but failed to suppress a snort. "I'm sorry, this is—" She burst into laughter.

"It's not funny."

"I'm sorry, I'm sorry. It's just…the fucking luck, right? I haven't seen him in person since he was still all growth-spurt gangly and awkward looking. He's the last person I expected to render anyone speechless, even if he did get hot."

I buried my face in my hands and groaned.

"Aw, Mouse, it's gonna be okay." She patted my back. "I'm ordering us another round. You need it."

My head sank to the bar and I whimpered. It was going to take a whole lot more than another round to calm my nerves, and I couldn't afford another one, anyway. "I want to go home, Iz."

I didn't mean our apartment, and she knew it, but she pointedly ignored me. "Okay, let's go then."

Once we were outside, she slung her arm around me as we walked toward the nearest T stop.

"Ugh. Why am I such a goober?" I slumped into her shoulder.

"Oh, sweetie, you're not a goober." She was trying to soothe me, but I wasn't falling for it. "You're not. Even if you were, he didn't seem to mind."

"He thought I was an interesting specimen of social awkwardness," I grumbled.

Izzy talked me down the whole way home. When we got back, she poured me a shot of bourbon and sent me to bed. I slept in fits and starts between frustratingly vivid dreams. Dreams of Matthew's fingers wrapped around my wrists, my hips, my thighs, holding me hard enough to bruise. The phantom scrape of stubble along my inner thigh woke me, throbbing and desperate in a way I hadn't felt in years. I'd barely been able to choke out a single word in the five minutes he'd been in front of me, and suddenly he was playing a starring role in a half-baked, rough sex fantasy that had come barreling into my psyche. I was almost too distracted by being so turned on to wonder what the hell that said about me.

Since I'd been unceremoniously dumped by my college boyfriend two weeks before graduation, few romantic opportunities had turned to zero inclination. I could barely remember the last time I'd had sex, except that it was disappointing, and I'd gotten used to celibacy. For the most part I'd come to a state of detente with my vagina. I would ignore its existence, except as necessary for health and hygiene, and my libido would play dead. It had been working out for us quite well for the last six years, and I had no intention of changing the agreement now, no matter how intense the false sense memories of his hands on my skin were.

In the morning, I flopped on the couch with a cup of coffee to begin my new routine of frantically sending resumes, filling out applications, and dragging around the apartment while checking my email every five minutes hoping someone, anyone, would call me for an interview.

I had packed my tiny Vermont life into the back of my car without even a hint of a job waiting for me. Izzy had dangled a new city, a new life, in front of me and I jumped. I would never escape if I didn't make a run for it now. I would live and die there. I would end up married to my childhood best friend, Will, and have his babies there. I left whatever didn't fit in my trunk either curbside or in my parents' basement. I had never done anything that could be described as reckless or irresponsible, but fuck that, I was going to be someone new.

While Izzy provided a steady stream of encouragement

that people were probably on vacation, nothing happened in August, once we were past Labor Day something would turn up, days went by with no responses. Rattling around the apartment staring at my email and refreshing job sites day after day started to get to me. What felt wild and free for about a week started to feel stupid and scary as days bled into weeks and my bank balance kept inching toward zero.

When my mind wasn't occupied with vague terror at having to go home, it had developed a frustrating habit of conjuring up Matt. Vague terror was almost preferable. I had a ridiculous crush on a man I had barely been able to speak one word to. I was like a teenager pining over a guy I'd seen once, all fluttering in my stomach and hot blushes in my cheeks, though my dreams were for a decidedly more mature audience. I had woken up aching and damp on far too many mornings since I'd clapped eyes on him. But this was my MO, after all. Get weirdly stuck on someone as a distraction for the constant feeling of impending doom, and then, as my ex had so charmingly put it, cling to them like a life raft until I drowned us both. He was a peach, and maybe not entirely wrong, even if the way he said it haunted me for years.

Was my brain getting dirty on me instead of having stress dreams that I couldn't hack it in the city and I'd have to go home in shame to bus tables at the Penalty Box? Probably. In that respect, graphic dreams of being held down and fucked by a hot near-stranger seemed like a pretty good coping mechanism. Especially when the likelihood of finding a real, live distraction from my anxieties seemed pretty small.

THREE WEEKS INTO SEPTEMBER, way past Labor Day and mythical hiring managers' returns from summer vacation, I confessed to Izzy that I didn't think I'd be able to stay.

"It was my brilliant idea that you move in with me. I'd be

paying the rent here anyway. It's not a big deal if you can't for a while."

"No, I'll go home. I shouldn't have come down here without having a job first. I'm not a charity project, Izzy. I can't take your money. I need to do this on my own."

"It's not taking my money, Mouse. You're family. You're staying in my spare bedroom while you look for a job, which is a normal thing family does for each other. Besides, you take care of me. Who else is going to make sure I'm fed and there are no sentient molds living in the back of the fridge?"

I rolled my eyes at her. Left to her own devices, Izzy would live on cereal and takeout straight from the contain-ers, which she inevitably forgot about. "You're disgusting, you know that, right?"

"That's why I have you." She grinned impishly. "Some-thing will turn up. When it does, you can pay rent, within reason, but until then, will you please stop worrying about it?" She set her plate on the coffee table and pulled me into a hug.

"Thank you," I mumbled into her shoulder.

Never mind that in my family, if you didn't move out when you turned eighteen, you started pitching in to help the household. But no matter how many years we had known each other, explaining to Izzy how the rest of the world lived generally produced a shrug and a pat on the head.

"What did I say, young lady?" She pulled back and gripped my shoulders, glaring at me with one eyebrow cocked, but I could see the corner of her mouth twitching as she held in her laugh.

"Oh, fuck off, Izzy. I hate feeling like a mooch, you hate that I feel that way. Let's call it even." I shrugged her hands off my shoulders and turned back to my dinner.

"Deal."

The following week, I finally got a contract job doing

basic data entry. It was barely more than a stopgap to my bleeding savings and made no promises of employment beyond a six-month window to complete the project, but it was something, and Izzy wanted to celebrate before I started on Monday.

"We should invite Matt."

"Izzy."

"What? Molly says he doesn't get out much, practically lives in his lab."

"He certainly seemed to have friends when we saw him out that time at the bar."

"Oh, come on. We've barely been out, and I know you think he's hot, but he's a nerd too. What happened to new town, new Mouse?"

I grimaced. I had been failing at Project Don't Be a Shut-in. "Fine. Invite him. For one beer, Izzy."

"One beer."

FRIDAY NIGHT, we were camped at a table in a semi-crowded bar waiting for Matt, who was running late, my stomach doing backflips while I willed my brain to empty of the mental images of him naked that I'd been entertaining for the better part of six weeks. I'd barely met him, knew nothing about him. But the way he'd looked at me that night, like he was studying me, like he could systematically pull me apart then put me back together again, did something to my insides. I wanted him to take me apart. Maybe he could put me back together into something new.

He strode in on his long legs, wearing fitted, dark jeans and a somewhat worse-for-the-wear, olive-green waxed canvas jacket. The thick strap of the messenger bag slung over his shoulders emphasized the breadth of him. His hair was mussed, like he'd been running his hands through it—or like someone else had been tugging on it. I nearly choked as my deeply unhelpful psyche reminded me of all the times I'd dreamed of being the one doing the tugging. With his face between my legs.

Fuuuuuuuuuuck. Stop it. Stop it right the fuck now. I'll spend my first paycheck on a vibrator if this will just stop.

Why, yes, I was making desperate bargains with my vagina. Because that makes sense. I didn't have time to hide under the table or make for an exit before he spotted us and started over, but I thought about it. Hard.

As he got closer, I wondered how long I had to stay before I excused myself to go climb out the bathroom window. Our eyes met. My brain screeched to a total halt. He gave me a satisfied, predatory smirk, holding my gaze like a challenge, and he wanted to win this time. The gears of my brain whirred back to life, and I looked away first as he got to the table. Izzy stood to give him a hug.

"Good to see you."

"I'm glad we could tear you away from work," Izzy teased.

He let go, set down his bag, and shrugged out of his jacket, revealing a plain black T-shirt stretched over his lean, muscled frame.

"I'll go get a drink. Do you need another round?"

"I think we're good. You good, Mouse?"

"Mm-hmm," I squeaked. I wished she wouldn't call me Mouse in front of new people, especially not in front of guys like Matthew. In my head, he was Matthew. He didn't seem like a Matt. Matt was Molly's nerdy older brother, Matthew was more fitting for the man who'd walked up to our table.

I could see Izzy plotting as he headed back to the table with his beer in hand. "Don't leave me alone with him, Izzy. Seriously. Please?"

"I'm going to use the restroom." The words were out of

her mouth before he'd even fully sat down. I smacked her thigh as she passed me.

He clearly knew what Izzy was up to and had the grace to shake his head into his beer.

"Jolene, nice to see you again." We were back to that predatory look. He knew he could chew me up, spit me out, and I wouldn't make a peep in protest. Hell, I'd probably even offer myself up as a sacrifice, given the chance.

"Matthew." I kept my voice as even as possible.

"Matthew. I like it." He smiled at me, and my stomach fluttered wildly at the notion I had pleased him. "I've never met a Jolene before."

"My mom is a Dolly Parton fan." I shrugged and rubbed a water ring on the table. "Kind of weird to be named after a home-wrecker. And my middle name is Mae. Nana had a conniption when she found out I was named after not one, but two 'women of low morals.'" Awesome. I was babbling.

Matthew laughed anyway and rescued me by changing the subject. "You know Izzy from college?"

"Uh-huh. We were roommates." I kept my eyes down, picking at the label on my beer bottle. I didn't trust myself to look him in the eye and speak at the same time.

"She said. You've stayed close, obviously. I know Izzy's getting her master's, but what brought you to Boston?"

There was no answer to his question that didn't involve a long, detailed history of my family, the fact that I'd never left my hometown before, my fear of becoming a crazy cat lady, and hey, why not throw in the part where I had panic attacks about little things like leaving the house and meeting new people, but I had to say something. "She asked me to come."

"You packed up and moved because she wanted you to?" I expected him to scoff like I was nothing more than Izzy's willing pet, but he sounded intrigued.

"I don't know." I really, really didn't. "I'm not usually impulsive. I think she caught me at the right moment."

He raised one dark eyebrow. "Oh?"

I blushed furiously. "I needed a change."

I shifted in my seat. The conversation felt less like polite small talk and more like an interview every time he opened his mouth. Thankfully, Izzy returned from the bathroom and saved me from Matthew's scrutiny. I could feel his gaze on me as I sipped my beer and stripped the label while he and Izzy caught up on the last ten-odd years. I kept my eyes on his hands, long-fingered and elegant, and the way they moved as he gave us the briefest description of his post-doctoral work at the hospital. He laughed when Izzy informed him that his sister was convinced he never left the lab and was grateful we were taking him out.

"Please, tell her you've saved me from a lonely Friday night with the cell cultures." He glanced at his watch. "But as it happens, I should get going." He stood and slid into his jacket before leaning over to kiss Izzy on the cheek. "It was great to see you, Izzy."

"You're not going back to work?" Izzy asked incredulously, even though she was as likely to be working on a Friday night as Matthew apparently was.

He quirked his perfect mouth but didn't otherwise acknowledge Izzy's question. "Lovely to see you again, Jolene."

I mumbled some sort of response as he headed for the door.

About the Author

Sionna writes award-winning sweet/hot HEAs, reads slower than she used to, thinks they deserve an award for not pulling over to pet the alpacas every time she drives by, drinks too much coffee, and has a weakness for expensive paint. They live in New England with their very patient spouse and very put-upon dog.

Acknowledgments

To the Rogue collective, for giving this story a home amongst so many amazing authors and stories in the series. And to my fellow *Rogue Passion* authors, who I am grateful to share this space with. Special shout-out to KD, Rebecca, Robin, and Jeanette for beta reading.

To my readers because I still can't believe you not only exist, but you tell other people to read my books. Thank you.

To my friends for their encouragement, wisdom, and hilarity. I raise my strawberry basil margarita to you.

To my family for their endless support.

To my spouse, who assures me that the world will not end, that we will be okay, and sometimes I believe him.